W9-ARP-775

THE SQUEAKY DOOR

THE SQUEAKY DOOR

Laura Simms
Illustrated by Sylvie Wickstrom

Crown Publishers, Inc.
New York

To my mother and father
and to Pura Belpré White
–L.S.

To my sister, Eva
–S.W.

Published by Crown Publishers, Inc., a Random House company,
225 Park Avenue South, New York, New York 10003.
CROWN is a trademark of Crown Publishers, Inc.

Manufactured in Hong Kong

Library of Congress Cataloging-in-Publication Data
Simms, Laura. The squeaky door/Laura Simms; illustrated by Sylvie
Wickstrom. p. cm. Summary: In this cumulative story, a little boy
overcomes his fear of the squeaky noise his door makes when his grandmother
closes it each night before he goes to sleep. [1. Fear–Fiction. 2. Noise–Fiction.
3. Bedtime–Fiction.] I. Wickstrom, Sylvie, ill. II. Title.
PZ7.S5919Sq 1991   [E]–dc20   89-23895

ISBN 0-517-57583-3 (trade)
     0-517-57584-1 (lib. bdg.)

10 9 8 7 6 5 4 3 2 1

First Edition

Once there was a little boy who was afraid of the sound of a squeaky door. He lived with his grandma in a house on a hill near a forest in Puerto Rico. Every single night the little boy got in his bed, pulled the covers up tight, and nestled his head on the pillow.

Then his grandma would come into the room and say, "Tonight, when I turn off the light and it's dark and I close the squeaky door to your room, are you going to get scared and jump under the bed and start to cry?"

The little boy always said, "No, not me."

And the grandma would answer, "Good. I am so old and so tired. I need my sleep."

But every single night when the room grew dark and she closed the squeaky door, the little boy got scared and jumped under the bed and started to cry. Night after night his old grandma had to take him into her room to sleep.

One night, the grandma said, "Are you going to be scared tonight?"

The little boy answered proudly, "No, not me!"

She said, "Good. Because tonight you are staying in *your* bed."

So she turned off the light. The room grew very dark and she closed the squeaky door. *Squeeeeeak!* The little boy got scared and jumped under the bed and started to cry—*waaa waaa waaa!*

The grandma came back into the room and she said, "You're driving me crazy. I can't get any sleep."

Then she got an idea. "I know. I'll put a cat in the bed so you won't be scared."

So the little boy got in the bed, and a cat got in the bed.

"Now," said the grandmother, "are you going to be scared?"

He snuggled up against the cat and said happily, "No, not me."

"Good," she said. She turned off the light and the room grew very dark. Then she closed the squeaky door. *Squeeeeeak!*

The little boy jumped under the bed and started to cry–*waaa waaa waaa!* And the cat jumped under the bed–*meow meow meow!*

The grandma came back into the room and sighed. "You are driving me crazy. I'm getting mad. What am I going to do? I know. I'll put a dog in the bed."

So the boy got in the bed. The cat got in the bed. And the dog got in the bed.

"Are you going to be scared now?" asked the grandma.

"No, not me," said the boy as he curled up beside the dog.

"Good," she said. "I need to get some sleep." She turned off the light and the room grew very dark. Then she slowly closed the squeaky door. *Squeeeeeak!*

The little boy got scared and jumped under the bed—*waaa waaa waaa!* The cat jumped under the bed—*meow meow meow!* And the dog jumped under the bed—*woof woof woof!*

The grandma came back into the room. "You're driving me crazy. I'm mad, mad, mad. I know. I'll put a pig in the bed."

The boy got in the bed. The cat got in the bed. The dog got in the bed. And the pig got in the bed.

The little boy pulled the covers up tight and put his arms around the pig.

The grandma yawned and asked, "Are you going to be scared tonight?"

"No, not me," he said, and he closed his eyes.

She turned off the light, and as soon as it was dark she closed the squeaky door. *Squeeeeeak!*

But the boy jumped under the bed and began to cry—*waaa waaa waaa!*

The cat jumped under the bed—*meow meow meow!*
The dog jumped under the bed—*woof woof woof!*

And the pig jumped under the bed–*oink oink oink!*

The old grandma came into the room and said, "I'm going to pull out every hair in my head. You're driving me crazy. I'm mad, mad, mad." Then she smiled and said, "I'll try a snake in the bed."

The boy got in the bed. The cat got in the bed.
The dog got in the bed. The pig got in the bed. And
the snake got in the bed.

"Are you going to be scared tonight?" she asked.

"No, not me," said the boy as the snake curled up
beside him.

Then the grandma kissed him good night and
turned off the light. The room grew very dark and she
closed the squeaky door. *Squeeeeeak!*

The boy jumped under the bed and started to cry—*waaa waaa waaa!* The cat jumped under the bed—*meow meow meow!* The dog jumped under the bed—*woof woof woof!* The pig jumped under the bed—*oink oink oink!* And the snake slithered under the bed—*hiss ssss ssss!*

The old grandma came back into the room. She switched on the light and sighed. "What am I going to do?" She sat down on the edge of his bed and whispered, "You are driving me crazy. I'm mad, mad, mad. We need to go to sleep."

Then all of a sudden she stood up and said, "Why didn't I think of this in the first place? I'll put a horse in the bed."

The boy got in the bed. The cat got in the bed. The dog got in the bed. The pig got in the bed. The snake got in the bed. And the horse got in the bed.

"Now, are you going to be scared tonight?"

"No, not me," the little boy said. And before he finished speaking, his eyes were closed.

So the grandma turned off the light and the room grew very dark. Then she carefully closed the squeaky door. *Squeeeeeak!*

But the boy opened his eyes and jumped under the bed and started to cry—*waaa waaa waaa!* The cat jumped under the bed—*meow meow meow!* The dog jumped under the bed—*woof woof woof!* The pig jumped under the bed—*oink oink oink!* The snake slithered under the bed—*hiss ssss ssss!* And the horse jumped under the bed—*neigh neigh neigh!*

And, with that, the bed collapsed!

The cat leaped out the window. The dog ran out the door. The pig broke down a wall. The snake slid under the floor. And the horse leaped and galloped and stamped until the whole house fell down.

So the boy and his grandma, the dog and the cat, the snake, the pig, and the horse had to move to a new house.

The new house had no squeaky door. And
there they lived happily, and quietly, ever after.

The Squeaky Door is adapted from a Puerto Rican folk tale I heard told in Spanish in 1968. I have adapted and retold this story to children all over the world and they, in turn, have made it their own. Here are some of the words as they would be spoken in Puerto Rico:

The Squeaky Door	La Puerta Chillona
little boy	el niño
grandmother	abuela
You're driving me crazy!	¡Me estás volviendo loca! (female) loco! (male)
dark	oscuro
the cat	el gato
the dog	el perro
the pig	el cerdo
the snake	la culebra
the horse	el caballo
No, not me.	No, fuí yo.
And there they lived happily, and quietly, ever after.	Y allí ellos vivieron felices, y tranquilos, para siempre jamás.

–Laura Simms

E
SIM

Simms, Laura *Copy 1*

The squeaky door

$12.95

DATE		
MAY 1 2 1992		
JUN 9 1992		
Harrison		

© THE BAKER & TAYLOR CO.